ROSEMARY WELLS

MAX'S

CHOCOLATE CHICKEN

VIKING

For Janet, who helped enormously

The full-color art for each picture consists of a
black ink drawing and a watercolor wash.

VIKING
Published by the Penguin Group
Penguin Putnam Books for Young Readers, 345 Hudson Street, New York, New York 10014, U.S.A.
Penguin Books Ltd, 27 Wrights Lane, London W8 5TZ, England
Penguin Books Australia Ltd, Ringwood, Victoria, Australia
Penguin Books Canada Ltd, 10 Alcorn Avenue, Toronto, Ontario, Canada M4V 3B2
Penguin Books (N.Z.) Ltd, 182-190 Wairau Road, Auckland 10, New Zealand

Penguin Books Ltd, Registered Offices: Harmondsworth, Middlesex, England

First published in 1989 by Dial Books for Young Readers, a division of NAL Penguin Inc.
This edition published in 1999 by Viking, a division of Penguin Putnam Books for Young Readers.

7 9 10 8 6

The Library of Congress has cataloged the Dial edition as follows:
Wells, Rosemary. Max's chocolate chicken.
Summary: When Max goes on an egg hunt with his sister,
Ruby, he finds everything but Easter eggs.
[1. Easter eggs—Fiction. 2. Easter—Fiction. 3. Rabbits—Fiction]
I. Title.
PZ7.W46843Masj 1989 [E] 88-14954
ISBN 0-8037-0585-9 ISBN 0-8037-0586-7 (lib. bdg.)

Viking ISBN 0-670-88713-7

Manufactured in China
Set in 20 point Minister Book

One morning somebody put
a chocolate chicken in the birdbath.

"I love you!" said Max.

"Wait, Max," said Max's sister, Ruby.
"First we go on an egg hunt.
If you find the most eggs, then you
get the chocolate chicken.

"And if I find the most eggs, then I get the chocolate chicken," said Ruby.

Max went looking for eggs,
but all he found was a mud puddle.

Ruby found a big yellow egg.
Max didn't find any.
"No eggs, no chicken, Max," said Ruby.

Max went looking again,
but all he found were acorns.

Ruby found a blue egg.
"Max," said Ruby, "pull yourself together.
Otherwise you'll never get the chocolate chicken."

So Max went looking with Ruby.
Ruby found a red egg with green stars.
Max found a spoon.

Ruby found a gold egg with purple stripes
and a turquoise egg with silver swirls and
a lavender egg with orange polka dots.
Max found some ants.

Then he made ant-and-acorn pancakes.
"Max," said Ruby, "you'd have trouble
finding your own ears if they weren't
attached to your head."

Ruby counted her eggs.
"I'm the one who's going to get the
chocolate chicken, Max," said Ruby.

But Max ran away.

And hid.

The birdbath was empty.

"Where are you, Max?" Ruby called.
Max ate the chicken's tail.

"I see you, Max!" said Ruby.
But she didn't.
Max ate the chicken's head.

"I'll give you half the chocolate chicken, Max!" yelled Ruby. Max ate the wings.

Then he popped out of his hiding place.

"Max," said Ruby, "how could you do this to me?"

"I love you!" said Max.